For Lilly, love you always.

Special thanks to Moms Who Write, who provide great feedback, support, and encouragement, and my cover critique group, both on FB.

First edition 2022

Summary: Santa sets the record straight and explains he is a magical being and is able to change his skin color, size, and style, which is why he looks different each time we see him.
ISBN 9798367840773

Illustrations created using digital paint and ink.

A Santa For EVERYONE

nicole
kimball
ostrowski

I've been hearing stories,
and I'm here to set the record straight.
We have to talk about my magic,
and there's no time to wait.

I thank you for listening
to all I have to say.

I don't want you to think I only look one specific way.

You see, sometimes I'm aglow,
with skin of peachy pink,
and I wear a long coat of red and white—
but I change more than you think!

Sometimes my skin may not look
the way you are used to seeing.

It may be shades of dark or light;
after all, I'm a magical being!

So I may be black, white, or tan—
my face flush from the snow or sun.

My hair is mostly gray or white,
usually down, but sometimes in a bun!

And I change my clothes each day,
like you should be doing, too.
I have many gorgeous garments,
in a variety of hues.

So you may see me out there,
in rosy red, cool blue, or white.

Some days I wear green and gold,
an outfit that's out of sight!

I can also be many different
heights and sizes...

...so I can sneakily deliver
lots of fun surprises!

If you have seen me around,
you may now fully understand...

...how I move through tiny spaces without getting stuck in a jam.

I stretch myself with elf magic,
so I get in easily.

And then I quietly place your presents
under the Christmas tree.

Next time you see me, remember,
I may have grown or shrunk in height.

I may be in glasses, wearing a wreath,
or using a cane that night.

I may be shaped more like a rectangle,
triangle, oval, or square.

And my head may have lots of
waves and curls
or hair that is barely there!

Sometimes I speak in another language, and you may not understand it.
That's because I speak to many children who live on this beautiful planet.

So if I don't look the exact same way
each time I'm near...

...just remember, I'm magical
and often change how I appear!

I love and represent all children;
they are part of magical me.

Which is why I don't appear just one way—
look around, you will see!

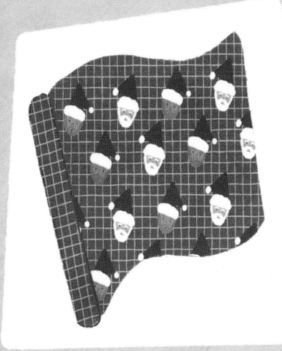

NICOLE KIMBALL OSTROWSKI is an indie
picture book writer and illustrator from Maryland.
A SANTA FOR EVERYONE is her third picture
book. She made her debut with I'M PICKLES
PINKERTON THE TOAD... APPARENTLY, followed
by SOME DAYS HE GROWLED. Her daughter is
often her muse. Nicole is looking forward to
creating her next picture book.

Printed in Great Britain
by Amazon

32807493R00021